BABY LEMUR

Susan Hellard

Piccadilly Press • London

Cover by Nicole Stanco and Louise Millar
Designed by Louise Millar

Printed and bound in Belgium by Proost
for the publishers Piccadilly Press Ltd,
5 Castle Road, London NW1 8PR

3 5 7 9 10 8 6 4 2

A catalogue record for this book is available from the British Library

ISBNs: 1 85340 541 8 paperback
1 85340 546 9 hardback

*Susan Hellard is an acclaimed illustrator who lives in North London. Her
illustrations have brought to life a myriad of characters, including Dilly the
Dinosaur. Sue won the Jean Piaget Award with Anita Harper for **Just a Minute** for
best integrated text and artwork.*

To David and Caroline
for providing a suitable habitat

When Liam was born, he was very tiny.
He cuddled his mother all day
and all night.

Liam and his mother lived at the very top of a tree.
His mother sang to him, and fed him, and
hugged him to her warm tummy.

When Liam was a bit bigger, his mother
put him on her back.
"Hold on to my back, little one," she said.
"You'll be safe there."

Liam's mother moved carefully through the trees.
At first Liam was terrified by the huge, scary jungle.

Slowly Liam grew bigger and braver.
And then he had great fun!
He and his mother soared from branch to branch.
They jumped over trees, and swung down from vines.
And all the time, Liam shouted, "Faster, faster!
Higher, higher!"

One day Liam's mother said to him,
"You're really quite big now, little one.

"Why don't you try things for yourself,
like the other little lemurs?"

The other little lemurs were playing games like
'Pull the Tail' and 'Hunt the Berry'.
Liam wouldn't join in. He didn't want to leave his
mother. He clung to her back and wouldn't let go.

But Liam's mother was firm. She knew that it was time for Liam to grow up. And so she took him off her back.

Liam didn't like this one bit. He sat down and howled. Then he banged his feet on the ground. Finally he lay very flat and refused to move.

But his mother didn't take any notice.
Finally Liam started to feel bored.
He could see the other young lemurs leaping
and playing and running. Suddenly Liam said
to himself, "I want to do those things too."
And he reached out and . . .

. . . SWUNG!

He soared over trees,

he swung down
from vines,

and he leaped
over branches.

One day he even did a double somersault,
which his mother had never tried.

Before long he was doing the same things as all the other little lemurs. Soon he forgot about being scared. He went higher and higher – to the very top of the tree.

And every night when the sun
went down and the moon rose, he
climbed up to his mother, and she
cuddled him in her warm fur.
He knew that whatever he did, or
wherever he went, she was always
there for him to come back to.

FACTS ABOUT LEMURS

Lemurs are primates (like humans).

Lemurs only live on the island of Madagascar. It is thought that their ancestors accidentally crossed to the island from Africa on clumps of vegetation which floated down the rivers and across the sea.

Lemurs eat fruit, leaves, flowers and insects.

Ring-tailed lemurs are roughly cat-sized and have the Latin name *lemur cattas*. They have a variety of calls – one of which is a miaow, which they use to greet each other.

Lemurs live mainly in the jungle canopy, but do go down to the ground, and enjoy sunbathing.

There are about 50 different varieties of lemur, ranging from species tiny enough to fit into an eggcup to those weighing over 7kg.

Lemurs give birth in August and September. They usually have only one baby, occasionally twins.
The baby lemur sits upright on its mother's belly.
After 2–3 weeks the baby climbs on its mother's back.
After 3 weeks the young lemur climbs about alone.
After 4 weeks the young lemur eats its first solid food.
After 6 months the young lemur is completely independent.

Lemurs live in troops of 15–20 adults. They remain with their troop for life.